THE
SNOWBEAR

words & pictures

When Iggy and Martina
went to bed, everything
was the same as usual.

But snow came in the
night.

Snow. Then more snow.

And when Iggy looked out
of the window, the whole
world was white.

Their mom told them,
"Make a snowman if you want.
But be careful because the hill
is too steep and slippery."

Martina said, "I'm shivering!"

Iggy slipped right over because the path
was icy! Martina almost slipped over
because she was laughing so much!

They made a snowman.

But their snowman looked
more like a snowbear.

"He looks happy to be made,"
said Martina.

And it was true.

"Now let's slide down the hill!" said Iggy.

"It's too steep and slippery," said Martina.

"We can do it!" Iggy told her.

And they did.

They slid and bumped even faster
than they thought they were going to.

The cold wind made their faces tingle.

The sledge kept going ... down the hill
... and into the trees.

Into the woods.

The air felt even colder.

It seemed they were
never going to stop.

But they did.

Nothing moved except
for one grey pigeon.

"I want to go home,"
said Martina.

"So do I," said Iggy.

He got off the sledge and
tried to pull it back the way
they'd come.

But Mom was right.
It was too steep and slippery.

The pigeon clapped its wings.
Then it was gone.

Standing between two trees
was a wolf.

Iggy and Martina looked at it.

The wolf looked back.

Its eyes were cold as icicles.

Then there was a sound. Something was coming.
The wolf turned its head. The three of them stared.

It was the snowbear!
He was lolloping down
the hill towards them.

The wolf backed off. It turned tail.

And it was gone.

Then the snowbear
picked up the children.

It picked up the sledge.

And it carried them home.

"Thank you for helping!"
Iggy said.

But the snowbear didn't say anything.
It just went back to where they'd made it.

When Mom came to find them, she asked,
"What have you been doing?"

"We made a snowbear," Iggy told her.

"And he came alive!" said Martina.

"He's lovely," Mom smiled.
"And he'll take a long time to melt."

But the next day, the weather was warm. And the snowbear wasn't there.

"Where is he?" asked Iggy.

"He could have melted already," Martina told him. And maybe she was right about that.

"Or he could have gone back in the woods and he's alive down there," said Iggy.

And maybe he was right about that.

Quarto is the authority on a wide range of topics.

Quarto educates, entertains and enriches the lives of
our readers—enthusiasts and lovers of hands-on living.

www.quartoknows.com

Text copyright © 2017 Sean Taylor
Illustrations copyright © 2017 Claire Alexander

First published in 2017 by
words & pictures, Part of The Quarto Group
6 Orchard, Lake Forest, CA 92630

A CIP record for the book is available from the Library of Congress.

ISBN: 978-1-91027-743-0

1 3 5 7 9 8 6 4 2

Printed in China